SEEING IN SLOW MOTION

Seeing in Slow Motion

A
THOUGHT-PROVOKING
COLLECTIBLE
SHORT STORY

Walter the Educator

Silent King Books

SILENT KING BOOKS

SKB

Copyright © 2024 by Walter the Educator

All rights reserved. No part of this book may be reproduced in any manner whatsoever without written permission except in the case of brief quotations embodied in critical articles and reviews.

First Printing, 2024

Disclaimer
This book is a literary work; the story is not about specific persons, locations, situations, and/or circumstances unless mentioned in a historical context. Any resemblance to real persons, locations, situations, and/or circumstances is coincidental. This book is for entertainment and informational purposes only. The author and publisher offer this information without warranties expressed or implied. No matter the grounds, neither the author nor the publisher will be accountable for any losses, injuries, or other damages caused by the reader's use of this book. The use of this book acknowledges an understanding and acceptance of this disclaimer.

A person has a freak accident one day and starts seeing in slow motion. He takes his newly discovered ability to the baseball field and becomes the greatest baseball player to play the game.

It was a typical summer day in Greenville, the kind where the sun blazed so fiercely it seemed to melt the asphalt and the air hung thick with the scent of freshly cut grass and sizzling barbecue. Jack WaMorton, an unassuming clerk at the local hardware store, went about his daily routine with the same predictable rhythm he had for years. Life had always moved at a steady, uneventful pace for Jack, and he had grown accustomed to its monotony.

Seeing in Slow Motion

That fateful day began no differently. Jack rolled out of bed, stretched, and wandered to the kitchen to fix himself a cup of coffee. He glanced out the window, squinting at the brilliance of the early morning sun, and sighed. His life had been an endless loop of early mornings, tedious workdays, and solitary evenings spent in front of the television. But today, fate had something extraordinary in store for him.

Seeing in Slow Motion

As he strolled to work, Jack's mind wandered. He thought about his childhood dreams of becoming a professional baseball player, dreams that had withered over the years as reality took its toll. He reached the store, greeted his boss with a nod, and began unpacking a shipment of garden tools. Lost in thought, Jack hardly noticed the peculiar, almost tangible tension in the air.

Seeing in Slow Motion

The accident happened in a blur. One moment, Jack was stacking shovels, and the next, he was on the floor, an excruciating pain radiating from his head. He had slipped on a stray wrench, hitting his head on a metal shelf as he fell. Darkness swallowed him, and he drifted into unconsciousness.

Seeing in Slow Motion

When Jack awoke in the hospital, the world seemed different. At first, he couldn't pinpoint what had changed. His head throbbed, and the room spun slightly, but beyond the physical discomfort, there was something fundamentally altered in his perception. It wasn't until a nurse walked in, her movements languid and dreamlike, that Jack realized what had happened. Time, it seemed, had slowed down.

Seeing in Slow Motion

The doctors were baffled. They conducted countless tests, but everything appeared normal. Jack's brain scans showed no signs of lasting damage, and his vitals were stable. Yet, for Jack, the world now moved at a crawl. Each second stretched into what felt like minutes, each minute an eternity. He could see the flutter of a hummingbird's wings in intricate detail, the fall of a single raindrop from the sky, and the subtle shifts of expression on people's faces as they conversed.

Seeing in Slow Motion

At first, this newfound ability was disorienting. Jack struggled to adapt, overwhelmed by the sheer volume of information his brain was processing. But as days turned into weeks, he began to find a strange beauty in his altered reality. The world had become a symphony of motion and detail, a dance of colors and shapes that he had never noticed before.

Seeing in Slow Motion

One evening, as Jack sat on a bench in the park, watching children play baseball, an idea struck him. He remembered his childhood passion; the hours spent dreaming of hitting home runs and making impossible catches. With his new perception of time, he wondered if he could rekindle that lost dream.

Seeing in Slow Motion

Jack started visiting the local batting cages. At first, he was rusty, his swings clumsy and uncoordinated. But with each session, he began to harness his ability. He could see the ball as it left the pitching machine, tracking its every rotation and trajectory. Hitting it became almost effortless. The ball seemed to hang in the air, waiting for his bat to connect with it.

Seeing in Slow Motion

Word of Jack's extraordinary talent spread quickly. Local scouts and coaches came to watch, their skepticism turning to awe as they witnessed his prowess. It wasn't long before Jack was invited to try out for the Greenville Minor League team. He accepted with a mixture of excitement and trepidation, knowing this was his chance to turn a freak accident into something remarkable.

Seeing in Slow Motion

On the field, Jack was unstoppable. He read pitchers like open books, predicting their throws with uncanny accuracy. His fielding was equally impressive; he moved with a grace and precision that left his teammates and opponents in disbelief. As Jack climbed the ranks, his reputation grew. He became known as "The Timekeeper," a player who seemed to control the very fabric of time.

Seeing in Slow Motion

Jack's journey to the Major Leagues was meteoric. Within a year, he was playing for the New York Yankees, his name on the lips of every baseball fan in the country. Sports analysts marveled at his stats, comparing him to the legends of the game. But beyond the numbers, it was Jack's seemingly supernatural ability that captivated the public's imagination. How could a man hit with such precision, field with such agility? Rumors and speculation swirled, but Jack kept the truth to himself, knowing that revealing his secret would only lead to more questions and possibly end his career.

Seeing in Slow Motion

In the big leagues, Jack faced new challenges. The competition was fiercer, the stakes higher. But his ability to perceive time in slow motion gave him an edge that no one else had. He continued to break records, leading his team to victory after victory. Fans packed the stadiums, eager to witness the magic of The Timekeeper.

Seeing in Slow Motion

Despite his success, Jack remained humble. He never forgot the life he had left behind; the days spent stacking shelves and dreaming of a different future. He used his fame and fortune to give back to his community, funding youth sports programs and mentoring aspiring athletes. He knew how fragile dreams could be, and he wanted to help others keep theirs alive.

Seeing in Slow Motion

One day, after a particularly intense game, Jack sat alone in the locker room, reflecting on his journey. He thought about the accident that had changed his life, the strange twist of fate that had turned an ordinary man into a legend. He realized that while his ability had given him incredible power on the field, it had also taught him to appreciate the small moments, the fleeting beauty of everyday life.

Seeing in Slow Motion

As Jack's career progressed, he faced the inevitable challenges of aging. His reflexes, once lightning fast, began to slow. He found himself relying more on his experience and intuition than his extraordinary perception. But even as his physical abilities waned, his love for the game remained undiminished. He continued to play with the same passion and dedication that had driven him from the beginning.

Seeing in Slow Motion

In his final season, Jack announced his retirement. The news sent shockwaves through the baseball world. Fans and players alike paid tribute to the man who had redefined the sport, celebrating his remarkable achievements and the legacy he would leave behind. On his last game, the stadium was packed to capacity, the air thick with emotion.

Seeing in Slow Motion

As Jack stepped up to the plate one final time, he took a deep breath, savoring the moment. The pitcher wound up, and in that instant, time seemed to slow even further. Jack saw every detail, every nuance of the ball's movement.

Seeing in Slow Motion

He swung, connecting with a satisfying crack. The ball soared into the sky, a perfect arc that seemed to hang in the air forever. The crowd erupted in cheers as it cleared the fence, a fitting end to a legendary career.

Seeing in Slow Motion

Jack rounded the bases, his heart full of gratitude and pride. He had lived a dream that few ever realized, transforming a freak accident into a story of triumph and inspiration. As he stepped onto home plate, his teammates lifted him onto their shoulders, carrying him off the field to a standing ovation.

Seeing in Slow Motion

In the years that followed, Jack remained a beloved figure in the world of baseball. He wrote a memoir, sharing his extraordinary journey and the lessons he had learned along the way. He continued to mentor young players, passing on his knowledge and passion for the game. And though he no longer saw the world in slow motion, he carried with him the profound understanding that life's true beauty lay in the moments that seemed to stretch on forever.

Seeing in Slow Motion

Jack WaMorton's story became a legend, a testament to the power of resilience and the magic that can be found in the most unexpected places. He had taken an accident, a twist of fate, and turned it into a gift, proving that sometimes, the greatest victories come not from the things we seek, but from the surprises life throws our way.

Seeing in Slow Motion

Years passed, and Jack WaMorton's legend only grew. His story became a beacon of hope for countless individuals; an example of how life's unpredictable turns could lead to extraordinary outcomes. Though Jack had retired from professional baseball, he remained deeply involved in the sport, dedicating his time to various philanthropic efforts and staying connected with the community that had always supported him.

Seeing in Slow Motion

One of his most cherished projects was the establishment of the "Timekeeper Academy," a state-of-the-art training facility for young baseball players. Located in Greenville, the academy quickly gained a reputation for producing some of the most skilled and disciplined athletes in the country. Jack's unique perspective on the game, combined with his deep love for teaching, made the academy a resounding success.

Seeing in Slow Motion

At the academy, Jack emphasized the importance of mindfulness and focus, drawing from his own experiences of seeing the world in slow motion. He taught his students to appreciate the subtle nuances of the game, to find beauty in the smallest details, and to stay present in the moment. His lessons went beyond baseball, instilling in his students a sense of resilience and a belief in their own potential.

Seeing in Slow Motion

One particular student stood out to Jack. A young boy named Ethan, who reminded Jack of himself at that age—full of dreams and raw talent but also struggling with self-doubt. Ethan was a natural athlete, with a keen eye and quick reflexes, but he often let the pressure of expectations get to him. Jack took Ethan under his wing, spending extra hours working with him, sharing stories from his own journey, and encouraging him to trust in his abilities.

Seeing in Slow Motion

Ethan's progress was remarkable. Under Jack's mentorship, he flourished, not just as a player but as a person. He learned to channel his nervous energy into focused determination, to see every challenge as an opportunity for growth.

Seeing in Slow Motion

By the time Ethan graduated from the academy, he had become one of the most promising young players in the country, earning a scholarship to a prestigious university and eventually being drafted into the Major Leagues.

Seeing in Slow Motion

Jack watched with pride as Ethan's career took off, seeing in him the continuation of a legacy he had helped to build. But for Jack, the greatest reward was knowing that he had made a difference in Ethan's life, just as so many people had made a difference in his own.

Seeing in Slow Motion

As Jack settled into his later years, he found joy in the simpler things. He spent time with his family, took long walks through the park, and enjoyed the quiet moments of reflection that had become so precious to him. He often thought about the accident that had changed his life, the strange gift it had given him, and the incredible journey that had followed.

Seeing in Slow Motion

One autumn afternoon, as the leaves turned golden and the air grew crisp, Jack found himself back at the old baseball field where it had all begun. He stood at the edge of the outfield, watching a group of children playing a pickup game. Their laughter filled the air, a sweet reminder of the pure, unadulterated joy that baseball could bring.

Seeing in Slow Motion

As he watched, he noticed a boy struggling at the plate, much like he had in his early days. The boy's face was scrunched with concentration, his knuckles white as he gripped the bat. Jack smiled, feeling a familiar tug at his heart. He walked over to the boy, kneeling down to meet his gaze.

Seeing in Slow Motion

"Hey there," Jack said gently. "Having a tough time?" The boy looked up, his eyes wide with recognition. "You're Jack WaMorton!" Jack chuckled. "I am. But today, I'm just a guy who loves baseball. Mind if I give you a few tips?"

Seeing in Slow Motion

The boy nodded eagerly, and Jack took him through the basics, showing him how to relax his grip, how to keep his eye on the ball, and how to swing with confidence. The boy listened intently, absorbing every word.

Seeing in Slow Motion

"Remember," Jack said, "it's not just about hitting the ball. It's about enjoying the game, staying focused, and believing in yourself. You've got this."

Seeing in Slow Motion

The boy's next swing connected with the ball, sending it soaring into the outfield. His face lit up with joy, and he turned to Jack, beaming. "Thank you, Mr. WaMorton!"

Seeing in Slow Motion

Jack's heart swelled with pride. "You're welcome, kiddo. Keep practicing, and you'll be great."

As he walked away, Jack felt a deep sense of fulfillment. He had come full circle, from a young boy with dreams of greatness to a legend of the game, and now to a mentor, passing on his wisdom to the next generation. His journey had been filled with twists and turns, triumphs and setbacks, but through it all, he had found his purpose.

Seeing in Slow Motion

In the twilight of his life, Jack WaMorton knew that the true measure of his success was not in the records he had broken or the fame he had achieved, but in the lives he had touched and the dreams he had helped to nurture. He had taken a freak accident, a twist of fate, and turned it into a story of hope and inspiration. And as long as there were young players stepping up to the plate, ready to take their shot, his legacy would live on.

Seeing in Slow Motion

One night, as Jack sat on his porch, gazing up at the stars, he felt a profound sense of peace. He had lived a life beyond his wildest dreams, filled with love, passion, and purpose. And though he no longer saw the world in slow motion, he cherished every moment, knowing that each one was a gift.

Seeing in Slow Motion

As he closed his eyes, a gentle breeze rustled the leaves, carrying with it the sounds of a distant baseball game. The crack of the bat, the cheers of the crowd, and the laughter of children filled the air, a timeless symphony that reminded Jack of the beautiful, unpredictable, and extraordinary journey that life could be.

Seeing in Slow Motion

And in that moment, Jack WaMorton, The Timekeeper, smiled, his heart full, knowing that he had made every second count.

Seeing in Slow Motion

ABOUT THE CREATOR

Walter the Educator is one of the pseudonyms for Walter Anderson. Formally educated in Chemistry, Business, and Education, he is an educator, an author, a diverse entrepreneur, and he is the son of a disabled war veteran. "Walter the Educator" shares his time between educating and creating. He holds interests and owns several creative projects that entertain, enlighten, enhance, and educate, hoping to inspire and motivate you.

Follow, find new works, and stay up to date
with Walter the Educator™
at WaltertheEducator.com

www.ingramcontent.com/pod-product-compliance
Lightning Source LLC
LaVergne TN
LVHW051925060526
838201LV00062B/4694